Weird Wolf

Weird Wolf

Margery Cuyler
Illustrated by Dirk Zimmer

A TRUMPET CLUB SPECIAL EDITION

Published by The Trumpet Club
666 Fifth Avenue, New York, New York 10103

ISBN 0-440-84810-5

This edition published by arrangement with
Henry Holt and Company, Inc.
Designed by Maryann Leffingwell
Printed in the United States of America
November 1991

10 9 8 7 6 5 4 3 2 1

*To Richard Hadden,
the creator of Murrr-DAH!
—M.C.*

Contents

1. Itch! Itch!

Itch! Itch!

I woke up feeling as if I had been attacked by a swarm of mosquitoes. I reached up to scratch my cheeks. Hair was sprouting out of my chin like weeds! Was I having a nightmare? I turned over, hugged my pillow, and tried to go back to sleep.

But now my arms were itching. And my stomach and legs.

I leaped out of bed, fell over my skateboard, and ripped off my pajamas. I looked down. Hair was growing all over my body! It glistened in the moonlight streaming through the window.

I ran into the bathroom and switched on the light. I looked in the mirror. Instead of seeing myself, nine-year-old Harry Walpole, I was looking into the face of a wolf! My breath was coming in big gulps, only it sounded like panting. My tongue was red and shiny, and it was hanging out of the side of my mouth.

I began to shake. My worst fear had come true. I was turning into a werewolf, just like my grandfather! My mother and father had tried to hush up the family scandal for years. But I'd finally got the truth out of Dad. Whenever the moon was full, my dad's father would become a werewolf. He'd roam the countryside, looking for red meat. When my grandmother found out, she tried to shoot him with a silver bullet. Dad never told me what happened after that.

I'd read about how werewolves can run in families, often skipping generations. First my grandfather, now me. And probably my grandchildren and great-great-grandchildren, too. The thought made my fur stand on end.

But something else was bothering me. Hunger! I craved a rare, juicy hamburger. Even twenty rare, juicy hamburgers. I licked my chops and headed downstairs. There was just one place that would satisfy me. McDonald's.

McDonald's was over a mile away, but it took me only a few minutes to get there. I could run as fast as the cars moving along Route 16. Maybe I was going crazy. But I couldn't think about that now. I didn't have room in my brain for anything but hamburgers.

As I reached McDonald's, the smell of sizzling red meat teased my nostrils. I began to drool, soaking my front paws. How was I going to order twenty hamburgers? I opened my mouth to test my voice. A long howl came out. It was so loud and eery that I jumped. All the neighborhood dogs began to bark. I felt like I was inside the dog pound. I shut my mouth and the howling stopped. I'd have to watch that.

The smell of hamburgers was making me feel faint. I had to eat something soon. Maybe I could pretend I was a dog. In the mirror I had looked like a German shepherd. I was so hungry, I was willing to try anything. Even begging.

I sat down by the front door and waited for somebody to come along. I was in luck. Abby Horowitz, from my third-grade class, was walking across the parking lot with her father.

2. Poor Doggie

Abby's nightgown was hanging down below her jacket. She was also wearing a pair of nerdy orange slippers. Her dad must have wanted to treat her to a late-night snack and gotten her out of bed. Her mom had died when she was little. I guess Mr. Horowitz didn't like to cook. I often saw him and Abby eating at McDonald's after he finished work.

In school Abby had a crush on me. I could tell because she was always doing stuff to get my attention. She'd ask me to be her partner in art class. Or get me to sit next to her in assembly. Or butt in front of me in the lunch line. And she liked to boss me around. "Harry, get me some more Jell-O," or "Harry, sharpen my pencil." She was a pain, but she was my only hope right now.

As she and her dad got closer, I concentrated hard on making my ears droop. It felt weird, like I had socks hanging down the sides of my head. Then I wagged my tail weakly. That felt weirder, like my rear was attached to a whisk broom.

"Poor doggie," said Abby.

"That 'poor doggie' looks vicious to me," said her father.

"I think he's cute," said Abby.

"You think all animals are cute," said Mr. Horowitz. "Come on, you said you were hungry."

He quickly steered Abby past me and through the front door. Soon they came back with bags of Big Macs, Chicken McNuggets, and fries. The inside of my mouth felt drippy. I flopped my tongue out and whimpered.

"He's hungry," said Abby.

"He looks well fed to me," said Abby's dad. Then he added, "I'm sure his owner will find him soon."

"What if he's been abandoned?" said Abby. "He doesn't have a collar on."

My ears perked up. Was this the Abby I

knew? She was acting *awfully* nice.

"People leave unwanted dogs on the highway all the time," she added.

Mr. Horowitz sighed.

"I'll tell you what," he said. "If he's still here at breakfast time, I'll call the vet. They might know if someone's looking for him."

Satisfied, Abby took her father's hand. They climbed into their car. I watched as they drove out of the parking lot.

My stomach gurgled. It felt as hollow as an empty goldfish bowl. I craved a Big Mac. And it might be hours before I'd get one.

Suddenly the side door opened. A boy in a McDonald's uniform came out with a huge plastic garbage bag. The aroma of hamburger meat reached my nostrils. The boy hurled the bag into a dumpster, then headed back to the kitchen.

I ran to the dumpster and leaped over the edge. I landed on bags of leftover cheeseburgers, hamburgers, orange juice, and Coke. I was in heaven. I ate until I thought I might burst. Then I did what any normal, self-respecting animal would do.

I fell asleep.

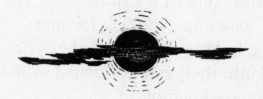

3. Maybe It Was a Ghost

When I woke up, the sky was rosy pink. It must be just past dawn, I thought. I didn't know where I was. Then I smelled garbage. I stood up, rubbing my eyes. Suddenly the events of last night rushed into my head. I shivered as I remembered the wolf's face in the mirror. The garbage bags shifted beneath me, and I grabbed the side of the dumpster. I looked down and saw that I was a boy again. But I didn't have any clothes on! I thought of how I'd left my pajamas on the floor by my bed. I should never have taken them off.

I began to shake from embarrassment as well as from fear. My knees trembled and my teeth chattered like castanets. I had to get home before school started. Mom and Dad would kill me if they discovered I was missing. Even worse, they might shoot me with a silver bullet if they found out I'd been a werewolf!

Frantically I looked around to see if I could cover myself with anything. All I could find was a McDonald's take-out bag. It was too small to do much good, but it was all there was. Holding it against me, I stumbled over the slippery garbage bags and jumped to the pavement.

I began to run home. A lonely car honked as I jogged along Route 16. I blushed to the roots of my hair. I'd never felt so humiliated in my whole life.

As I got nearer to our street, a familiar car turned onto the highway. I couldn't believe it. It was Abby and her father. They were probably on their way back to McDonald's for breakfast. With one hand I grabbed a fallen tree branch and covered my front like a fan. With the other hand I held the McDonald's bag still closer. I looked around quickly for a hiding place. Luckily there was a large rhododendron bush by the side of the road. Quickly I leaped behind it.

Mr. Horowitz slowed down and stopped the car. He rolled down the window and stuck out his head. He squinted at the bush where I was hiding. I held my breath, and my heart stopped. If I crouched any lower, I'd dig a hole in the ground. I put the branch over my head. Now Abby was stretching her neck out the other window.

"How strange," said Abby's father. "I could have sworn I saw a naked kid jump into this bush."

"Maybe it was a ghost," said Abby in a shaky voice.

"Nonsense," said Mr. Horowitz. "It looked sort of like that kid in your class. You know, the one with the red hair."

"You mean Harry Walpole?" asked Abby.

I groaned.

"Yes, that's the one," said her father.

"No way," said Abby. "Harry's much cuter. Besides, that kid was too skinny to be Harry."

I blanched. I wasn't *that* skinny.

"I must have been seeing things," said her father.

He shrugged and turned on the engine. As he drove away, Abby was still hanging out the window, staring at the bush.

That had been close! Now, if I could only get home without bumping into someone else. I ran another mile and turned into my street. I dashed the two blocks to our house, dropped the branch, and raced to our front door. It was locked, so I lifted up the dining-room window. I dived through as fast as I could. Just then a siren went off. The burglar alarm! I'd forgotten all about it.

Mom and Dad came tumbling downstairs. Their hair stuck out in all directions. They'd obviously just woken up. Crouching, I backed toward the kitchen. Frantically I tried to cover my body with my hands and arms as well as with the McDonald's bag.

"Harry!" screamed Mom. "What on earth is going on? Where are your pajamas? What were you doing outside without any clothes on?"

Dad raced to the kitchen and called the police.

"Don't come," he shouted into the receiver. "It was a false alarm. . . . What? . . . No, my son Harry set it off by mistake."

Dad slammed down the phone, while Mom kept firing questions at me.

"Where are your pajamas? Why were you outside?"

I could never explain it to her. I couldn't even explain it to myself. Besides, if I told my parents the truth, they'd keep me home from school. And drag me to a psychiatrist. And there was no telling what Dad would do, since he couldn't even deal with his own father being a werewolf.

By now the McDonald's bag was torn. Clutching what was left of it, I hobbled to the hall closet and grabbed the first coat that I saw. Mom's down jacket. I threw it on. It barely covered the tops of my legs. I inched toward the stairs, feeling like a walking sleeping bag.

Dad came back into the hallway.

"What is going on?" he asked. His voice crackled with excitement and alarm.

"I don't know," I said. "I went to sleep last night, like always. When I woke up this morning, I was standing on the porch without any clothes. I must have been sleepwalking."

Well, I was *almost* telling the truth.

Mom put her arm to her head. "I wonder if the neighbors saw you." She collapsed into a chair.

I *had* to get upstairs before they asked any more questions, so I did the only thing I could think of. I sneezed. Five times in a row.

"Oh, dear," said Mom. "You probably caught cold."

"Go upstairs and get in the shower," said Dad. "Before you get really sick."

If he only knew how sick I was. Mentally, that is. Or was I?

"Calm down, dear," Dad was saying to Mom. "Let's fix some coffee. I'm sure Harry *was* sleepwalking."

"Either that or we have a lunatic on our hands," said Mom.

Muttering, they went into the kitchen.

I ran up the stairs and jumped into the shower. I scrubbed my body with the washcloth, trying to rub away all werewolf traces. I wished I could wash away the memory, too. Then I checked my face in the bathroom mirror for werewolf hairs and threw on some clothes.

I raced back down to the kitchen and grabbed an apple. I knew the school bus would be coming any minute.

"See you," I called to Mom and Dad as I put on my jacket.

I rushed out the front door and got to the bus stop just as the bus was pulling up. The door swung open. My eyes bugged out. Abby Horowitz was sitting at the front of the bus. She was grinning from ear to ear. Oh, no! What if she *had* recognized me earlier without my clothes? After all, now she'd had time to think about it. I wished I could disappear.

"I saved you a seat," she said.

I groaned. What would happen now?

4. What If Werewolves Got Ticks?

"Sit down and help me with my math home-work," ordered Abby.

She was back to her obnoxious self. But I didn't mind. I was just relieved she hadn't recognized the "ghost" she had seen earlier.

I looked around the bus. Tim was beckoning to me from the back. He's my best and only friend, even though we're opposites. I love to read. He hates to. He's a big talker. I'm not. He's tall and dark. I'm short with red hair. But we're both crazy about baseball.

I brushed past Abby. "I can't," I said. "Tim's waiting for me."

Abby's shoulders slumped, but just for a moment. Then she said brightly, "I'll save you a seat on the way home."

"My mom's picking me up," I lied. I walked quickly to the back of the bus. Then the strangest thing happened. I suddenly wanted to climb up beside Tim and lick his face! It was really weird. But the urge passed quickly. I wished I could tell him about last night. But he'd never believe me. He'd think I was crazy.

I sat down and asked him about the plastic cup that was on his lap.

"Ticks," he said. "I saved them from last summer. Mom and I plucked them out of Snoozer's ears and drowned them in ammonia."

"How come you're bringing them to school?"

"For my science report," Tim answered. "Our topics are due today."

I stuck my finger into my ear and poked around. What if werewolves got ticks? I couldn't feel any. Maybe I'd write my science report on wolves. After all, I'd already had some experience, and I still needed a topic.

"Where's your lunch?" asked Tim.

Dad had been so confused earlier, he'd forgotten to pack it. Usually he packed mine and Mom's. Poor Mom. She'd go hungry too. I wondered if there was a cafeteria in her bank office.

"I forgot it," I said quickly.

"You can share mine," said Tim. "My mom made chili for dinner last night, and I get all the leftovers for lunch. Even cold, it's great."

"Thanks, but no thanks." I wasn't really into *cold* chili.

Tim opened his lunch box and took out a bag of potato chips.

"I'm hungry," he said, ripping open the top.

Suddenly the mouth-watering aroma of chili hung in the air. Was I imagining it or had my powers of smell improved? The chili was in a container with a seal-top lid. So how come I could smell it?

"Can you smell the chili?" I asked.

"No, why?" said Tim. He closed his lunch box and the smell went away. I shook my head and held out my hand for some potato chips.

"No reason," I answered as the school bus turned into the parking lot. But to myself I was thinking, That chili smell *was* really strong.

*   *   *

All morning I had a hard time concentrating. If only last night had been a nightmare! But things kept happening that made me realize it hadn't. Little things, like smelling the chili in Tim's lunch box. Or wanting to lick his face on the bus. During recess I saw an old bone by the school fence. I wanted to pick it up in my mouth. Even though I was tempted for only a second, it freaked me out. I guess the werewolf spell hadn't completely worn off. I had to figure out how to break it. Permanently. So, during lunch hour, I went to the library.

I read everything I could about werewolves. I found out that people changed into them on the night of the full moon. I also learned that people in the Middle Ages thought the werewolf came from the devil entering the body. The curse could be broken only if the werewolf spirit was exorcized. I thought about a movie I remembered Mom telling me about. It was called *The Exorcist.* It was the story of a girl who had an evil spirit living in her body. It had to be driven out, or exorcized. It sounded really scary. I wasn't going to go through that! Then I read about the other ways werewolves got back to their human forms.

I made a list:

1. Getting pierced with a knife.
2. Diving into water.
3. Putting human clothes back on while still a werewolf.
4. Getting set on fire.
5. Getting wounded in a fight.
6. Getting called by your human name while still a werewolf.
7. Getting killed with a silver bullet.

I knew for sure I didn't want to be killed, even as a werewolf. I immediately scratched out numbers one, four, and seven. That left numbers two, three, five, and six.

I'd have to try all of them the next time I changed into a werewolf—*if* I changed into a werewolf. I hoped it would never happen.

5. Dith-gush-ing

For the next few weeks I almost forgot about having been a werewolf. The symptoms had completely disappeared. Everything seemed normal. Tim and I joined the Coyotes, our local kids' baseball team. I did my science report on wolves. I earned five dollars planting grass seed for our next-door neighbor. I also avoided Abby Horowitz as much as possible.

On the first Saturday in April, Tim asked if I'd like to come over for the night. He said we could have pizza and watch a movie on the VCR. Tim's dad picked me up on his way back from getting the pizza. It was meatball and pep-pers—my favorite kind.

Tim, his mom and dad, his two-year-old sister Maria, and I had dinner at the kitchen table. Maria got more pizza on her face than in her mouth.

"Maria's disgusting," said Tim.

"Dith-gush-ing," said Maria.

"Doesn't she know what her mouth is for?" complained Tim.

"Mouth for," said Maria.

"Mom, does she have to repeat everything I say?"

"That's how toddlers learn to talk," said Mrs. Mendoza.

Maria picked up some pizza in both her fists and smeared it on her hair. Then she tipped over her milk, drenching Tim's pants.

"Let's get out of here," said Tim.

We made a quick exit to the den and the VCR. Tim and his dad had rented the movie *Ghostbusters,* which I'd already seen three times. Still, I was looking forward to it.

After I had been watching it for half an hour, my ears started itching. I scratched them. Then the bottoms of my feet got itchy. And my arms and neck. I looked out the window. A full moon was hanging in the sky like a large, shiny grapefruit. Why hadn't I noticed it before?

I sprang up from the couch and ran to the bathroom. I looked in the mirror. Yikes! My eyebrows were getting bushier by the second. Luckily Tim's mom had left a tube of lipstick by the sink. I quickly scrawled a message to Tim on the mirror: I JUST THREW UP. AM CLIMBING THROUGH THE WINDOW TO GET HOME.

I knew he'd think I was nuts, but there wasn't time to explain. Already hair was sprouting out of the backs of my hands. In a few minutes they'd be paws. I lifted the window and squirmed through. My clothes made me feel itchier than ever. I tore them off and threw them in the bushes. Then I headed for the road. I had to find some red meat. I was starving.

6. Queenie

I headed for McDonald's. Just as I was turning up Chestnut, I heard loud yapping. It was coming from a ranch house on my left. A door banged open, and a woman's voice scolded, "You have to sleep in the yard tonight. Maybe then you'll stop whining so I can get some sleep!"

The most beautiful golden retriever I had ever seen ran outside. Her fur shimmered in the moonlight like a polished copper penny. Her eyes glistened like two jewels. She raced across the yard. When she reached the fence, she stood still and lifted her nose. Then she lay down in the grass and started rolling around.

My heart was skipping beats and my body was trembling. I wanted to climb over the fence to make friends. But just then a small, ugly terrier streaked by. He was followed by a cocker spaniel and a large mutt. Suddenly dogs were coming from every direction. They were barking and yapping and running toward the fence.

A light bulb went on in my head: Get wounded in a fight, and you'll break the spell. I dashed after the other dogs. A growl rumbled like thunder in the back of my throat. My fur stood up on end like tiny knives. My eyes felt like they were on fire. I wanted to fight all of them. The ugly little terrier took one look at me and raced away, his tail between his legs. The other dogs stopped. The cocker spaniel bared his teeth. If Abby Horowitz and her father hadn't shown up, I hate to think what I might have done.

Abby's father had a hose with him. He started spraying me. I fell over. Some of my strength began to leave my body. Then I remembered: Dive into water, and you'll break the spell.

I leaped up and dived toward the hose, but Mr. Horowitz was aiming it at the other dogs. They were retreating, their legs moving in a blur. He shut off the valve, and my strength began to return.

The woman who owned the golden retriever had come outside. She was trying to pull the retriever to the kitchen door. The dog wouldn't budge. It kept looking over her shoulder at me and whimpering.

"Darn it, Queenie, you're the most stubborn dog I've ever met! But I can't blame you, poor thing. You're the prettiest dog in town."

Mr. Horowitz unlatched the gate and went into Queenie's yard. He pushed Queenie from behind while her owner pulled her from in front. Queenie was still looking at me. Her eyes were soft with love. But it was not to be. Within minutes she was safe inside the kitchen.

"Thank you, Frank," called her owner. "Come over for some coffee tomorrow morning." Then she closed the door.

I wanted to continue my trip to McDonald's, but someone was patting my head.

"I wish I owned a doggie like you," said Abby gently. "You look scary, but I know you're not. Your eyes are too friendly. Who do you belong to, anyway?"

She pulled a dog biscuit out of her pocket and held it in front on me.

"I think you're hungry," she said. "I carry these for my doggie pals. Maybe you can come to my house and dry off. I live over there."

She pointed to the red house in the lot next to Queenie's.

Even though my stomach wanted to go to McDonald's, my heart wanted to stay here. I wagged my tail. I took the dog biscuit between my teeth and chowed down. Maybe Abby wasn't such a nerd after all. Anyone who liked animals couldn't be that bad.

Suddenly Mr. Horowitz started running toward us. "Get away from that beast!" he yelled. "He's either mad or sick."

He yanked her away.

"He is not!" cried Abby. "He's just different."

Mr. Horowitz picked up a rock and threw it at me. Poor Abby. Her father was really weird. I scrammed before another rock could hit me.

7. One, Two, Three, Four

I spent the next few hours gorging myself in the dumpster behind McDonald's. Then I ran back to Tim's house. I fell asleep beneath the bushes where I'd thrown my clothes. When I woke up, I was happy to see I was a boy again. It was beginning to get light out.

I put my clothes on and got home before anyone was awake. This time I remembered to press the little hidden button that turned the alarm off. Then I let myself in with the key that was under the flowerpot by the back door.

Just as I was about to sneak to my bedroom, I heard someone coming down the back stairs. I recognized the muffled sound of Dad in his running shoes. Why did he have to pick *this* morning to jog? I knew he'd wonder why I was home when I was supposed to be at Tim's. I also knew that Tim had probably tried to call me. Mom and Dad had gone out for dinner last night, so with any luck he hadn't reached them.

For now, I had to hide. And quickly. There was only one closet in the kitchen, and it was jammed with cleaning stuff and canned food. So I did the only thing I could think of before Dad arrived in the kitchen: I dived under the table. As soon as he left for his jog, I'd write him a note. I'd explain that I'd come home early from Tim's and gone to bed because I felt sick, or something. Then I could call Tim later and tell him that I was feeling much better. Mom would miss out on the whole thing because she always sleeps late on Sundays.

As I was thinking, Dad walked over near the table and started his warm-up exerices. I could see him wriggling his ankles. I held my breath as he leaned down to touch his toes. "One, two, three, four . . ." he panted. His hands and head were going up and down like a yo-yo.

Suddenly he looked over. Our eyes locked. For a few seconds Dad's head and arms and hands disappeared. I gulped. My heart was

beating like a hammer. Then Dad's face came back into view.

"What are you doing under there?"

I was quivering with fear. Dad grabbed my arm and pulled me out from my hiding place.

"I thought you were at Tim's," he said.

"I was," I answered. "But I came home early. For breakfast," I added quickly.

"At six o'clock in the morning?"

I blinked. I had to lie. Again.

"See, Tim snores. And he talks in his sleep. It kept me awake all night. So I decided to come back here to get some rest. I thought you'd be mad, so I hid when I heard you coming downstairs."

"Mad? I'm not *mad*. Just surprised, that's all. You startled me. Tim's parents will worry when they find you missing."

"I left a note," I said. Well, I had, sort of, so I wasn't exactly lying.

"That's okay, then," said Dad. "At least you didn't sleepwalk again!"

Dad shook his head as he went outdoors. I shook mine as I headed up to my room.

I was lucky that Dad had been the first one up. Mom might not have swallowed my story so easily.

8. Nobody Turns Into a Werewolf

When I got to my room, I took out my getting-rid-of-a-werewolf list. There had to be something on it that would still work. I couldn't go on like this. I reread the list. Getting into a fight and diving into water hadn't been too successful. I crossed out numbers two and five.

1. ~~Getting pierced with a knife.~~
2. ~~Diving into water.~~
3. Putting human clothes back on while still a werewolf.
4. ~~Getting set on fire.~~
5. ~~Getting wounded in a fight.~~
6. Getting called by your human name while still a werewolf.
7. ~~Getting killed with a silver bullet.~~

Only numbers three and six were left. They'd be easy if I told someone my secret. But how could I? No one would believe me. Still, I'd have to think about telling Tim. He was the only person who might be willing to help me.

As I sat looking at my list, breakfast smells were filling my room. Dad was back from his jog and making bacon. The smell pulled me downstairs and toward the kitchen like a magnet. I started to drool. I wiped my mouth on my sleeve. Darn. The spell hadn't completely worn off.

The phone rang. I knew it was Tim. I scrambled back upstairs to get it. Luckily there was an extension in Dad's office.

"Are you all right?" asked Tim as soon as I picked up the phone. "I was worried when I found your message. I tried to call you last night, but no one answered."

"Mom and Dad were out, and I was asleep. I was exhausted. I think the pizza made me sick," I said. "I feel okay now," I added.

There was a pause. Then Tim asked, "Are you sure you're okay? You disappeared awfully quickly."

I swallowed hard. I had to tell him. Then he

could help me, and he wouldn't be suspicious anymore. I took a deep breath. I would tell him this afternoon.

"Can you come over after lunch?" I asked. "There's something we need to talk about."

Tim showed up in his Houston Astros T-shirt. His hat was on backward, and baseball cards were sticking out of his back pocket.

"Let's go sit in the tree house," I said.

I was carrying two Cokes, a bag of pretzels, and a Bible. We walked to the terrace out back.

"What's the Bible for?" he asked.

"I want you to swear, on the Bible, that you'll never tell anyone what I'm about to tell you."

Tim's eyes got as big as sand dollars. I set the Bible on the wooden picnic table. I placed Tim's hand on top.

"Do you swear?"

Tim held his breath.

"I swear," he said.

We trudged to the old tree behind the garage and climbed the ladder to the tree house. Then,

as the sun came through the cracks in the wood and speckled our arms, I told him my secret.

Tim drew a circle in the sawdust by his feet. He was quiet for a long time. Then he stood up quickly.

"I don't believe you," he said. "Nobody turns into a werewolf. Except in books and movies, maybe."

"Then how come I left so fast last night?"

"I don't know," said Tim. "But not because you were a werewolf. That's ridiculous!"

"It's true!"

"You're lying!" yelled Tim.

"I am not!" I yelled back.

"You are too!" said Tim. "I don't ever want to hear you talk like that again. You promise?"

He was clenching and unclenching his fists.

It was no use. He'd never understand.

"I can't promise," I said.

"Then I'm leaving," said Tim.

He practically flew out of the tree house.

9. Creep!

Abby saved me a seat again on the bus Monday morning. This time I sat down. After all, hadn't she stuck up for me in front of her father? Hadn't I seen another side of her when she'd offered me the dog biscuit? She was putting the finishing touches on a drawing in her notebook.

"Can I see?" I asked.

She tore out the picture and handed it to me. I almost fainted. It looked exactly like me as a werewolf!

"Isn't he beautiful?" she asked.

I squirmed.

"He's a stray," she said. "I feel sorry for him. Some family probably abandoned him on Route Sixteen. My dad thinks he's dangerous, but he's just lonely and hungry. What he really needs is a home and someone to love him. I'd take care of him, only my father won't let me."

Suddenly a hand reached over my shoulder

and grabbed Abby's picture. The hand belonged to Tim.

"What an ugly mutt," he said. "Or is it a wolf? It's so bad, I can't even tell."

"Hey, give that back!" said Abby. Tim wouldn't let go. The drawing ripped. I watched the two halves of my furry face float to the floor.

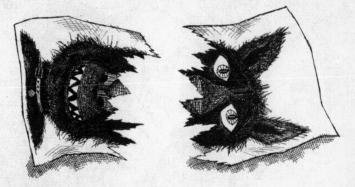

"Creep!" shouted Abby. She crossed her arms and glared at him. Her face was burning with anger.

I picked up the pieces of the drawing and handed them to her. For a minute Tim looked like he was sorry. Then he grabbed my arm and said, "Come on, let's sit in the back."

But I didn't want to. My friendship with Tim felt torn in two, just like Abby's drawing. For the second time in two days, he'd been mean. Even if he didn't believe my werewolf story, he didn't have to be *that* mean.

"Not unless you tape Abby's picture back together."

Tim looked at me and shook his head.

"No way," he said. Then he added, "You're no fun anymore."

He stomped to the back of the bus and grabbed George Miller's baseball hat. He started tossing it to the other kids.

I sat down next to Abby. "Too bad about your drawing," I said.

Abby looked away. "Thanks for sticking up for me," she said finally.

We rode for a while in silence.

Then Abby smiled. "Do you want to come to a barbecue at my house?"

"When?" I asked.

"The Saturday of Memorial Day weekend."

"Can't," I said. "That's when we play the last game of the season."

Abby bit her lip. Then her face brightened. "I know," she said. "I'll postpone the barbecue until a day that you're free."

I was beginning to like Abby, but this was going too far.

"Better not," I said. "When I'm not playing baseball, I'm doing chores around the house."

"Oh," said Abby. She looked sad. For a second I felt sorry for her.

"Tell you what," I said. "If the game gets rained out, I'll come."

Abby sat up straighter and grinned.

"I'll pray for snow," she said.

I looked out the window. We were passing McDonald's. My stomach started to growl. Or was I just imagining it?

10. Go-o-o-o-o-o, Harry!

It was Memorial Day weekend. I was getting ready for our last baseball game. If we won this one, we'd be league champs. The game was going to be tough. The Colts had only lost two games, and our team, the Coyotes, hadn't beaten them for several years.

I tied my shoes and went downstairs to our backyard. Dad was grilling chicken, and Mom had made nachos with hot sauce. She was sitting at the picnic table with her head in her hands.

"What's wrong?" I asked.

"Grammy phoned. She's in the hospital. The doctor put her in after she felt chest pains. Your father and I have to drive up to Austin. I'm afraid we have to leave after we eat."

"You mean you'll miss the game?"

My heart sank. I really wanted my folks to see me play. This was the big game of the season.

"I'm sorry, Harry," said Dad, "but Grammy

is all alone. She needs us."

What about me? I thought. I need you too. But I didn't say anything. I knew Grammy was lonely and probably scared. Hardly any of her friends were still alive. And my mom was her only child.

"I've arranged for a lady named Mrs. Morey to stay with you," said Mom. "She's supposed to be really nice. I got her from the agency. She's even supposed to like baseball, so we thought we'd encourage her to go to the game."

I couldn't believe it. Not only would Mom and Dad miss the game, but I was going to be cheered on by a stranger. What a bummer.

After our barbecue Mom went to pick up Mrs. Morey. When they came back, Mrs. Morey walked into the yard in a Houston Astros hat. She was also carrying an Astros tote bag.

"Hi, Harry," she said. "I'm really looking forward to seeing you play. Coach Colburn is a friend of mine."

She put up her right hand.

"Give me five," she said, and we traded high fives. I guessed we'd get along.

"We'll need all the luck we can get," I said.

"I'll meet you back here after the game," she said.

I picked up my baseball mitt and climbed onto my bike.

"Say hi to Grammy," I called to Mom and Dad. "I hope she's okay."

I pedaled toward the street. I felt an empty place in the bottom of my stomach. I was missing Tim. We used to bike together to all the games.

When I got to the park, Coach Colburn blew his whistle and called our team together.

"Keep your eye on the ball and don't swing for the fences," he said. "Concentrate. Remember those basics we worked on."

Tim was standing across from me. For a moment our eyes locked. Then he turned away.

Our team was up first. Tim hit a ground ball and made it to first. Then everyone else struck out, so we didn't score. By the seventh inning we still hadn't scored. The Colts were winning, two to nothing. I was up at bat. There were two outs. George Miller was on second and Tim was on third. I had to drive them home.

The butterflies in my stomach were getting worse. It was beginning to get dark, so I couldn't see the ball that well. And I was beginning to itch. Behind my ears. And on my hands and neck. I looked up. A full moon was starting to rise in the sky. Help! Not tonight! I couldn't be changing into a werewolf tonight! Why hadn't I paid more attention to the date? I frantically swung the bat. It cracked as it connected.

"It's a home run!" screamed Coach Colburn. I just stood there.

"Run!" yelled Tim, pushing me off home plate as he came in from third base.

So I ran.

As I headed toward first base, I began to pick up speed. I could hear the air whistling by my

ears. I cleared all three bases in a matter of seconds. I touched my face as I crossed home plate. Hair was sprouting on my forehead. I had to get out of here! I could hear the team cheering behind me.

"Go-o-o-o, Harry! Go-o-o-o-o, Harry!"

Then, instead of slamming into the bench for high fives, I ran all the way out of the park, tearing my uniform off as I went.

I could hear Mrs. Morey's voice behind me. "Harry! Where are you going? *Harry!*" I'd have to figure out something to tell her later. I was getting pretty good at lying.

My tongue flopped out of my mouth. My fur rippled in the wind. I looked over my shoulder, but I couldn't see the team. I was too far away.

Was my home run the game winner? There were only two more innings to go after this one. The Colts still had time to score. Could the Coyotes win without me? My worries began to fade as my stomach cried out for red meat. I raced toward McDonald's.

11. Weird Wolf

I began to drool as I thought about all the hamburgers being ordered on Saturday night. As I passed Chestnut Street, I caught a whiff of charcoal and . . . what was that delicious smell? Steak! My stomach growled. A charcoal-grilled steak was better than a McDonald's hamburger any day. I slowed down and turned into Chestnut Street. The smell was coming from behind the red house halfway down the block. That house looked familiar. Then I remembered. It was Abby's house. And this was the night of her barbecue.

My mouth was dripping. I craved a steak. I had to have it. Maybe I could try begging again. I knew Abby would feed me if her father wasn't around. I'd try anything for a bite of juicy, tender sirloin.

I reached the driveway and slouched behind the hedge. I sat down and peered through the bushes. Mr. Horowitz was shoveling some steaks off the grill and onto a platter.

He carried the platter to the picnic table, where ten kids from my class were seated. They were stuffing their faces with potato chips, pretzels, and salad. But my nose kept smelling those steaks. It was all I could do to keep from leaping over the hedge and devouring them.

Just as I was wondering what to do next, the phone rang and Mr. Horowitz went inside. I bolted from my hiding spot, landing on top of the platter. Sarah Scott's mouth fell open like a trapdoor. She took one look at me and fainted. The other kids shrieked, jumped up from the table, and started running. But Abby rushed over to me.

"My doggie. My nice, weird doggie!" she cried.

"Your nice, weird wolf!" yelled Joey Romano, who had shimmied up a tree.

"But he really *is* nice," cried Abby. "And he really *is* a dog. He just looks scary. He won't

hurt you. I know him."

Gradually Abby was able to persuade the kids to come back. Meanwhile I tore into the steaks, then whimpered for more.

"Oh, you poor thing," said Abby. "You're starving."

She put a bowl of potato chips and a dish of ice cream by my feet. I gobbled everything up.

"There's another raw steak in the cooler," she said.

She brought it over, feeding it to me from her hands. I wagged my tail and licked her fingers as I swallowed it whole. Then she went into the house. When she came back, she said, "I don't want you to disappear again, so I'm going to tie you up." She pulled a collar out of her pocket. "I found this at the dump," she said. "All these months I've kept it inside, in case my dad changed his mind about letting me have a dog."

I could have run away, but I didn't want to hurt her feelings. Not after all the food she'd given me. I could always escape later. I sat quietly while she fastened the collar around my furry neck and walked me to the garage.

"I'll keep you here until I have a chance to talk to Dad. I've *got* to talk him into keeping you."

She tied me to a hook inside the garage. Then she looked at me thoughtfully.

"You need a name." She paused in thought. "I know—I'll name you Harry. After my friend, Harry Walpole." She hugged me and kissed me on the nose. "You're a good dog, Harry." Then she went to the door.

"I'll be right back," she said. "I want to bring you some water."

It's lucky she left, because suddenly my body began to shake. My tail curled and uncurled. My ears flopped over. Everything started to get blurry. Before I knew what was happening, I passed out.

12. What Are You Wearing?

I must have fainted for only a second, because when I came to, Abby wasn't back yet. I was shivering, and the collar around my neck felt loose. I looked down. There I was, once more a boy. Abby had broken the spell! She had called me by my human name! I wanted to jump up and down and shout. But my problems were not over. I had no clothes on again, and I was tied by a leash to a pipe. I wondered how other werewolves dealt with this clothes problem. I was getting awfully sick of it. If Abby or my classmates found me now, I could never look them in the face again.

Quickly I undid the collar. Then I frantically looked around for some clothes. Tools, skis, and garden equipment were hanging from hooks on the walls. But there weren't any clothes. Then I noticed a few boxes in the corner. I ran over and tore open the top one. I pulled out some clothes, but I didn't have time to examine them. I heard the kitchen door slam. Abby was on her way back to the garage.

I held onto the clothes, closed the box, and dashed to the window. I barely had time to open it and dive through before Abby appeared.

I must have opened a box of costumes. I was holding a long, purple-velvet dress with shiny stars glued to it. It was the dress Abby had worn as Cinderella in the school play last fall. Normally I'd die rather than put on a girl's dress. But right now I had no choice. I pulled it over my head and stumbled into the shadows. The front must have had a hundred buttons. I barely had time to button the top three. The skirt was long, so I had to gather it up on each side in order to move. Otherwise I'd trip. This was almost as terrible as running around without any clothes on!

It had gotten really dark by now. I could see pretty well, though, because of the full moon. If I kept to the bushes and avoided streetlights,

I could make it back to where I'd thrown my uniform. Then I'd be safe.

It took me quite a while to get to the park. It was lucky that most of my classmates were either at Abby's or at the game.

I crept into the park the back way. I stumbled over to where I thought I'd thrown my uniform. It wasn't there! I got down on all fours and started grabbing at the grass. It had to be there! It just had to!

"Harry, is that you? What are you doing? I've been looking all over for you. And—" Then I heard a loud gasp. "*What* are you wearing?"

The voice was coming from behind me, and it was the voice of Mrs. Morey.

I leaped up, tripping over my hem. *R-r-r-rip!* The skirt began to tear, exposing my ankles, shins, and knees.

I thought Mrs. Morey would pass out on the spot. Her eyes were popping out of her face. Her eyeglasses were jumping off her nose.

Why did I always land in these impossible

situations? What could I tell her—that I'd changed from a werewolf into a boy who was in desperate need of his uniform?

"I— I— I— I can't explain it now," I blurted. "I have to get back to the game. I'll tell you what happened later."

She looked at me, speechless. Her eyes were still popping out of her face. In shock, she pulled something out of her bag. It was my uniform!

"Is this what you were looking for?" she managed to whisper. "I found it on the ground over there." She pointed to a nearby spot under some trees.

I grabbed the uniform from her outstretched hand and ran toward some bushes. I crawled behind them and quickly changed. Then I hid Abby's dress. I'd come back and get it later. I'd sneak it back into her garage some other time.

Leaving Mrs. Morey staring wide-eyed behind me, I walked toward the game. I needed time to figure out what to say to the team. Everyone would ask me why I'd run away.

13. Maybe It Was Just Nerves

As I reached the bleachers, my team was on the sidelines. Coach Colburn was smiling. My teammates were slapping one another on the back. Our team had won!

"Hey!" said Tim when he saw me. "That was some home run!"

Everyone rushed toward me.

"Nice going, Harry!"

"What a hit!"

"You won the game for us!"

Coach Colburn came over and put his arm around my shoulders.

"Too bad you had to leave. Tim told us about your stomach troubles. Are you all right now?"

I looked over at Tim. He winked. Did he know what had happened? Or was he trying to stick up for me so we'd be friends again? I'd have to ask him later.

I looked back at Coach. "Yeah, I'm okay.

Maybe it was just nerves."

"Speaking of eating, I'd like to treat you all to some hamburgers at McDonald's," said Coach. "Then I'll take you all home in the van."

"Whoopee!" yelled Tim.

"Let's go!" cried George.

"How about it, Harry?" asked Coach.

I didn't know what to do. I wanted to celebrate, but the thought of hamburgers made me sick. Still, this was the most exciting night of my life—hitting a game-winner and breaking the werewolf spell. I had *plenty* to celebrate. I could always order Chicken McNuggets or a fish sandwich.

"I'm coming!" I answered.

Just then Mrs. Morey walked onto the field. She looked at me strangely. Coach Colburn went up to her and grabbed her arms. "Isn't this great? We won. We beat the Colts!"

"Yeah, great," she said, still looking at me.

"We're going to McDonald's to celebrate," I said. "Coach will drop me off later."

"Where's your bike?" asked Mrs. Morey. "I might as well ride it home."

I reached into my pocket and gave her the key to my lock. I pointed to the fence.

"It's the black one with the Astros decals."

She looked pretty funny as she biked down the road, out of the park. But not as funny as I must have looked in my Cinderella dress.

14. His Name Is Harry

When I got home that night, I talked to Mom and Dad on the phone. They were thrilled that I had hit the winning home run. They said they'd be back the following night, since Grammy was all right. The tests showed that she had a heart problem called angina. But she wasn't in any danger. The doctor had given her pills to make her feel better.

Mrs. Morey never asked me about the Cinderella dress. Even so, I explained that I'd been conned into wearing it by a teammate who wanted to play a joke on Coach. I thought I should tell her something so that she wouldn't think I was crazy. After I told her my made-up story, she held up her hand.

"Some things are better left unexplained," she said. "I'd rather leave here tomorrow night remembering the fantastic home run you hit."

Tim came over the next day. He told me he was sorry he hadn't believed my werewolf story. "You have to admit, it was far-out," he said. "I still don't believe it, even though it was strange the way you disappeared last night."

"Thanks anyway for saying I was sick," I said. "It doesn't matter anymore that you didn't believe me. The spell has been broken. I won't ever talk about it again."

Tim looked at me and smiled.

"Friends?" he said.

"Friends," I answered.

That afternoon I biked over to the park and got Abby's Cinderella dress. Then I snuck into her garage and packed it in the box. I hoped she could fix the rip if she ever wore it again.

Before I got on my bike, I went up to her front door and rang the doorbell.

"Harry!" she said when she opened the door. "I heard you won the game yesterday!"

"I did," I said. "And I want to celebrate by taking you out for some ice cream."

She smiled so hard I thought her skin would split.

"Great!" she answered. "But first I have to show you something." She disappeared for a few minutes. When she came back, she was carrying a kitten.

"His name is Harry," she said. "Just like yours. Dad gave him to me this morning. I guess he wanted to make me feel better. Last night a stray dog I adopted ran away. Dad wouldn't have let me keep him anyway. He doesn't like dogs. But he *does* like kittens. Isn't Harry cute?"

"He is," I said. But to myself I thought, Kittens are cute, but they can't smell as well as werewolves. Or beg. Or run as fast.

But would I want a werewolf for a pet? No way.

When we got to the ice-cream parlor, Abby said, "I want a double scoop of pink bubble gum and chocolate-almond fudge. I want sprinkles and M&Ms on the top, but no Oreo

crumbs. My friend here will have the same.''

That was Abby. Bossy as usual. But somehow it didn't bother me. After all, how could I dislike her after she broke the spell? And how could I dislike anyone who named a cat *and* a werewolf after me?

I prayed there'd be no more werewolves in my family. But if I did end up with a werewolf for a grandchild, I hoped someone like Abby Horowitz would be around to help.